WHERE IS ROBIN?

LOS ANGELES

THIS BOOK
BELONGS TO:

....

....

CREATED & WRITTEN BY ROBIN BARONE
ILLUSTRATED BY RACHEL GOZHANSKY

THIS BOOK IS DEDICATED TO
The travelers who went before me, alongside me, and those yet to come.

ABOUT WHERE IS ROBIN?
We are a platform that uses adventure travel to teach children about the world.

Typeset in Revers.

Printed in China.

For sales inquiries, contact sales@diplomatbooks.com.

⠿ DIPLOMAT BOOKS

Diplomat Books
New York, New York

www.diplomatbooks.com

ISBN 978-0-9906310-8-8

Robin arrived on the West Coast of the USA by flight.
She was ready to experience Los Angeles
during the daylight.

"City of Angels, you are a gem to explore!
I am so excited that I arrived. Let's begin my tour!"

Immediately, Robin headed to the Pacific Ocean
and arrived at Marina Del Rey.
There were so many water sports available,
"I cannot wait to play!"

Robin picked out a board and declared,
"I think that I am a windsurfer!"
She cruised around the channels,
"I am pretty good for an amateur!"

In Venice Beach Robin joined the crowd
along the Ocean Front Walk.
She was skating so fast that she could not talk.

The path was crowded with animals and people alike.
Robin discovered that her legs could skate faster
than riding a bike!

The Philharmonic is housed
at the Disney Concert Hall.
As the orchestra's conductor, Robin had a ball.

This world-class destination
encourages a curiosity to dream.
Through Frank Gehry's vision,
anything is possible it would seem.

In Downtown Robin played in a Kings' hockey game.
As the left wing offensive, Robin found fame!

As she approached the goalie, Robin's focus was intense.
Her hockey skills were clever on the offense.

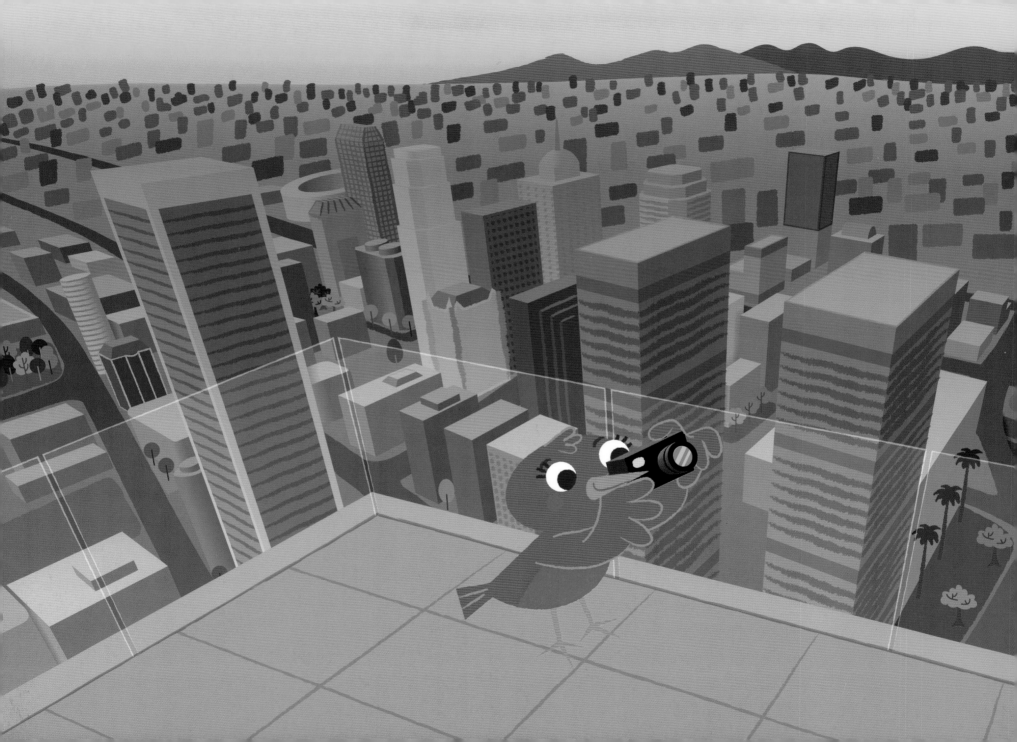

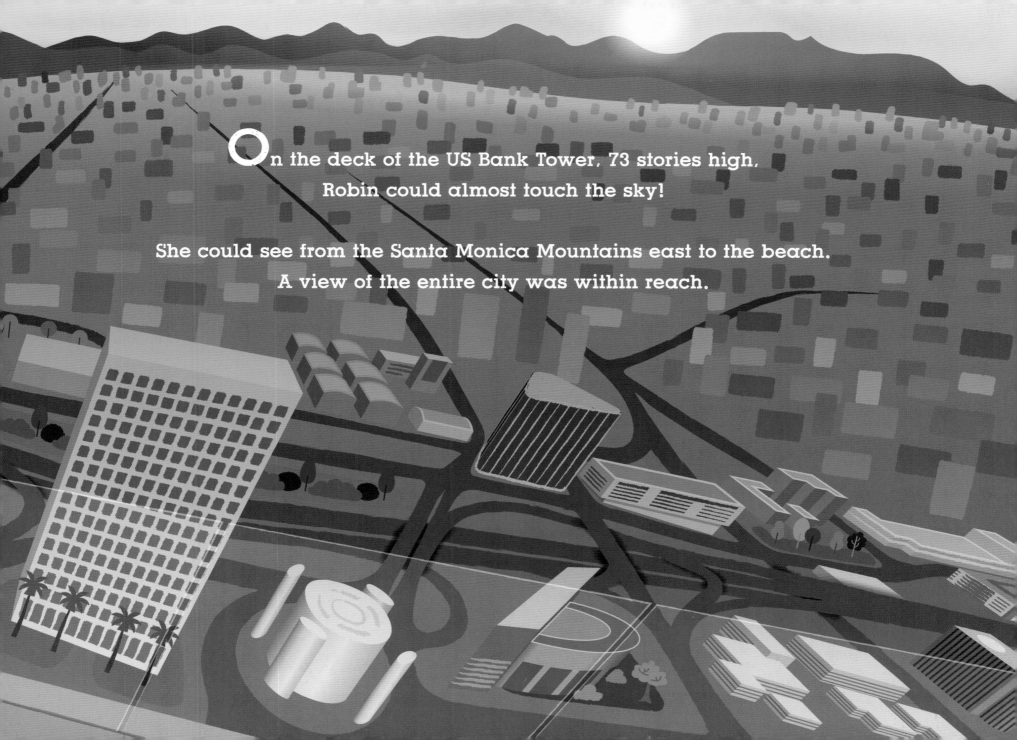

On the deck of the US Bank Tower, 73 stories high,
Robin could almost touch the sky!

She could see from the Santa Monica Mountains east to the beach.
A view of the entire city was within reach.

The Los Angeles County Museum of Art
is located on Wilshire Boulevard.
It is known for amazing jazz concerts in its courtyard.

The history of the world lies through the entrance of these doors.
Centuries of art can be found walking LACMA's floors!

DREAM. PLAN. GO. DREAM. PLAN. GO. DREAM. PLAN. GO. DREAM.

In Pasadena Robin headed to the Huntington Library
where the International Gardens are legendary.

She found herself transported to China and drinking tea,
and for a moment she saw how different life could be.

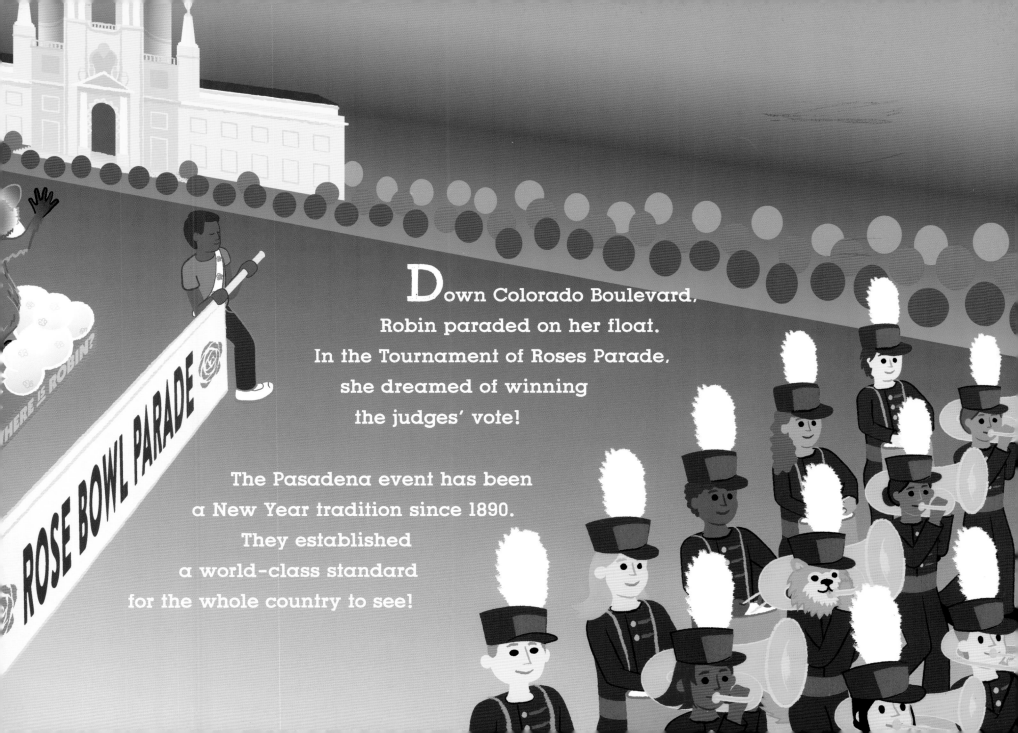

Down Colorado Boulevard,
Robin paraded on her float.
In the Tournament of Roses Parade,
she dreamed of winning
the judges' vote!

The Pasadena event has been
a New Year tradition since 1890.
They established
a world-class standard
for the whole country to see!

ROSE BOWL PARADE

WHERE IS ROBIN?

HOLLYWOOD

The Griffith Park Observatory is home to the Zeiss Telescope.
The best view of Los Angeles can be seen
from Mount Hollywood's slope.

The observatory is a leading place to explore astronomy.
Thanks to local friends it is open for everyone to see.

This spot is one of Robin's favorite places in the city
because it inspires imagination, dreams, and curiosity.

Along the Santa Monica Mountains
and onto Mulholland Drive,
driving along the winding road in Laurel Canyon
Robin felt alive!

This North-South roadway connects
the San Fernando Valley to Hollywood.
Its curvy roads go through a hilly neighborhood.

Who could be performing tonight at the Hollywood Bowl?
It looks like Robin and her Adventurers are on a roll!

With her debut at the largest outdoor stage in the United States,
Robin soon recognized that a musical career awaits!

Exploring Hollywood the local energy sparkled in Robin's eyes.
She enjoyed the day under California's blue skies.

Robin drove along Sunset Boulevard on her trip.
This road, which leads to Downtown, is also called the Strip!

Grauman's Chinese Theatre is located along Hollywood Boulevard.
This famous movie theatre looked like a scene from a postcard.

Living the dream along the Hollywood Walk of Fame,
Robin imprinted her wings to immortalize her name.

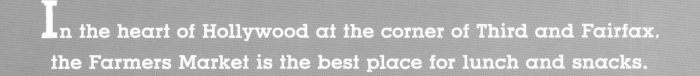

In the heart of Hollywood at the corner of Third and Fairfax,
the Farmers Market is the best place for lunch and snacks.

"Fresh food grown locally from farm to table."
While she ate lunch, Robin read the label.

Robin found herself on a tour around the set of a movie studio.
"I would like to act. Let's go!"

If Robin could act in a movie, a Western film came to mind.
She thought acting as a sheriff would be the best role assigned.

In the heart of Beverly Hills,
Robin walked along Rodeo Drive.
She was in a center where glamour
and fashion were alive.

VIA RODEO
N. RODEO DR
Fashion Forward
DREAM.
PLAN.
GO.
GIFTS GALORE
GIFTS GALORE
GIFTS GALORE
WHERE IS ROBIN?
1820

DREAM. PLAN. GO.

Robin arrived in the heart of Santa Monica and headed to the Pier.
Swimming, biking, and fishing were all near!

Robin boarded the cart of the solar panel ferris wheel.
From the view above, she understood the beach life appeal!

At the Getty Villa
Robin explored antiquities of Ancient Greece and Rome,
The Getty is a place where sculpture and art call home.

The vast art collection provided an opportunity for her knowledge to grow.
Standing in their courtyard, Robin experienced life in Europe centuries ago!

LOS
LIONES
CANYON
PARKER MESA OVERLOOK

On her hike over the Pacific Palisades in Los Liones Canyon,
Robin admired the view below along with her hiking companion.

Overlooking the city Robin began to meditate.
"This trip is amazing. This city is great!"

"My tour is complete. My time has come to an end.

There's no place like Los Angeles.
See you later my new friend."

Follow Robin's other adventures!

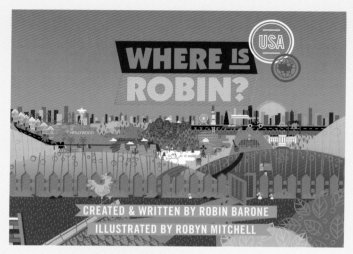

Where is Robin? USA
ISBN: 978-0-9906310-9-5

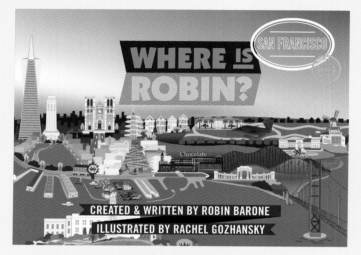

Where is Robin? San Francisco
ISBN: 978-1-946564-06-1

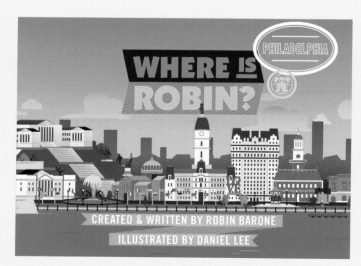

Where is Robin? Philadelphia
ISBN: 978-0-9906310-5-7

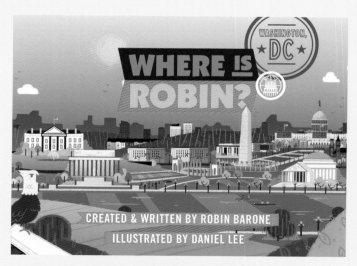

Where is Robin? Washington D.C.
ISBN: 978-0-9906310-6-4

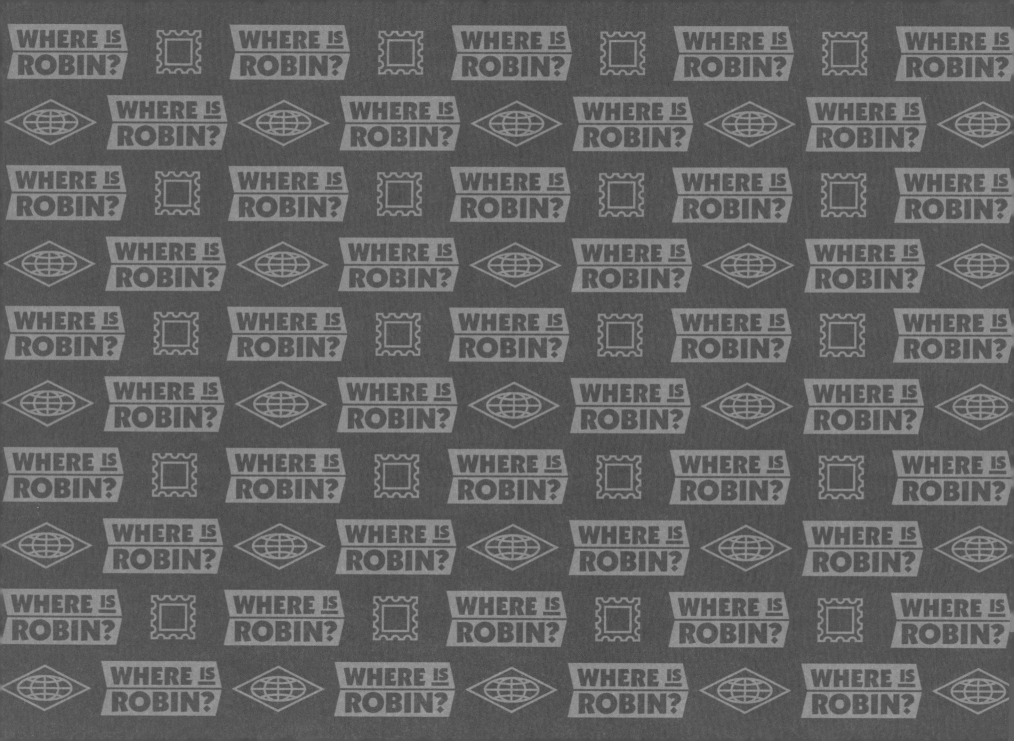

WITHDRAWN

WHERE IS ROBIN?

LOS ANGELES

BEACH
CITIES

11

210

9

PASADENA

UNIVERSAL

HOLLYWOOD

10

12

14

13
W. HOLLYWOOD

HOLLYWOOD /
CENTRAL L.A.

WESTSIDE

RODEO DR

17

BEVERLY
HILLS

15

7

19

16

10

5

SANTA
MONICA

21

CALIFORNIA
1

20

Atlantic
Ocean

18

10

4

6

5

3

2

405

BEACH
CITIES

DOWNTOWN /
L.A. METRO

110

NEIGHBORING
REGIONS

5

710

1

105

WHERE IS
ROBIN?